Tales of Africa

Retold Timeless Classics

Perfection Learning®

Retold by Nancy Tolson

Editor: Lisa Owens
Editorial Assistant: Berit Thorkelson
Illustrator: Laura Bryant

For information, contact:
Perfection Learning® Corporation
Phone: 1-800-831-4190 • Fax: 1-712-644-2392
1000 North Second Avenue, P.O. Box 500
Logan, Iowa 51546-1099

Paperback ISBN 0-7891-2857-8
Cover Craft® ISBN 0-7807-7851-0
Printed in the U.S.A.
8 9 10 PP 09 08 07 06 05 04

Table of Contents

ANANSE GETS OUT OF WORK

IT WAS PLANTING season. Ananse the Spider had come up with a brilliant idea. He declared that the work in the fields should be divided into two parts. One part should be worked by his wife. And the other part should be worked by his son.

Ananse's wife and son agreed. "We should both work in the fields," they said. "The planting will get done more quickly."

But they did not agree that the work should be divided in two. They wanted Ananse to work in the fields too.

Ananse reluctantly agreed to help. And he went off to bed to prepare for the next day. He declared, "I'll need my rest!"

The next morning, Ananse was just about to step out of the house. Suddenly, he fell ill. He fell down upon the floor. And he could not move from the spot.

Ananse kicked and screamed with pain. It seemed that a great lump had formed on his cheek.

"Where did that come from?" Ananse's wife asked.

"I don't know," he replied, in agony. "It just showed up while I slept."

Ananse's wife was very concerned. So she stayed behind for a while. She told her son to go on ahead. "I'll join you in the fields," she promised. "Just as soon as I make your father more comfortable."

She prepared a cozy resting place for Ananse. Then she set up fans nearby. And she cooked a large pot of Ananse's favorite soup.

Once Ananse had settled down and the soup was ready, his wife left.

As soon as she was out of sight, Ananse

jumped up from his resting place. He felt quite refreshed. And, surprisingly, he was no longer in pain.

Ananse was very hungry. He was so hungry that he ate all the soup in the large pot. He didn't even leave one small drop. Then the lazy spider lay around the house for the rest of the day.

In the early evening, Ananse spotted his wife and son returning home. He could see that they were both tired and very dirty from a hard day's work. When they stepped inside the house, Ananse fell ill again. The lump on his cheek was even larger than it had been that morning.

Ananse's wife and son were surprised that Ananse had gotten worse.

"The lump on your cheek has gotten bigger!" cried Ananse's son.

Ananse's wife took a closer look at the lump. She wondered where the lump had come from. And she wondered how to get rid of it.

"Let me touch the lump," said Ananse's wife. She touched it lightly with one finger. She was very careful.

Even so, Ananse cringed and screamed. "Such horrible pain!" he cried.

Ananse's son wanted to take a look at the lump too. He knew better than to touch it. So he slowly crept to Ananse's side. As he neared his father, the son tripped. And his hand accidentally slapped Ananse's cheek.

Ananse's mouth flew wide open. And out popped a big lime!

The lime rolled across the floor. And Ananse hung his head.

"All day long, we thought you were sick!" exclaimed Ananse's son.

"We did all the work. And you just lazed about the house!" shouted Ananse's wife.

Wife and son were very angry. They chased Ananse the Spider right out of the house. They didn't let him return until he promised to work in the fields by himself.

How Ananse got the work done and the crops in is truly another story.

A Tale from the Coast of East Africa

The Lion of Manda

A LION ONCE lived on an island named Manda. It was opposite an island named Shela. Every night, the lion roared so loudly that the people of Shela couldn't sleep.

A rich merchant grew very tired of hearing the lion roar each night. So he offered to pay $100 to a brave man. That man would have to travel to Manda. And he would have to sleep alone there for one night.

For a long time, no one accepted the merchant's challenge. Then one day, a poor young man heard the offer. He thought about it for a long time. And he told his wife about it.

The wife was very worried. She didn't want him to go to the island. She was afraid that he would be eaten by the lion. But she did understand how much they needed the 100 dollars.

"Go if you must, husband," said the wife.

The young man promised to stay safe. When evening fell, he took a small boat and paddled across the water to the island. Once there, he prepared a bed on the shore.

Now the young man's wife had followed him to the edge of Shela. She sat upon the shore directly across from her husband. And she built a small fire from sticks. Her husband could see her from across the shore.

The wife kept the small fire burning all night. This comforted her husband as he slept.

The next morning, the young man awoke. He had not been bothered by the roaring lion. He returned to Shela at once. And he headed straight to the rich merchant's house.

"I slept alone on the island of Manda," said the young man. "I've come to collect my reward."

The merchant refused to give it to him. He said, "You did not earn it. I know that your wife sat on the shore across from you. This removed your fear. So it doesn't count."

The young man was very upset. So he reported the merchant to the sultan.

The sultan called the merchant and the young man in to talk about the problem.

Again, the merchant stated why the young man had not earned the 100 dollars.

The sultan asked the young man if what the merchant said was true. The young man admitted what his wife had done.

The sultan wanted to stay in good favor with the rich merchant. So he agreed that the young man had not earned the 100 dollars.

The young man was sad and very confused about the sultan's decision. As he was leaving the sultan's palace, he bumped into a sage.

The sage noticed the young man's mood. And he wanted to know what had happened.

So the young man told him the entire story.

The sage said that he could get the 100 dollars for the young man.

"I'll give you one-third of the money for your help," said the young man gratefully.

The sage visited the sultan. He invited him to lunch in his home the next day. The sultan was never one to refuse food. And he happily accepted the invitation.

The sage rushed home to prepare for the sultan's visit. He decided to serve the meat of an ox. He put the meat in many pots. Then he gathered plenty of wood for the fires.

The next day, the sage arranged the many pots of meat on one side of the room. And he had made many fires. The fires burned directly across the room from the pots of meat.

The sage gave his servants instructions.

When the sultan arrived, he was escorted to the patio. He and the sage sat and talked for a while.

Later, the sage called out to his servants. "Check the fires and the meat," he said. The servants ran inside and did as they were told.

Noon had long since passed. And the sultan was feeling quite hungry. He was enjoying his visit. But his hunger was getting strong. So he asked, "How soon will the food be ready?"

The sage called to his servants again. He ordered them to check the fires. And to make sure that the meat was cooking properly. Then he tried to continue talking.

Well, the sultan was very hungry. He couldn't stand it any longer. He insisted that the meat must be ready by now.

The sage called to his servants. He asked whether the food was done. The servants replied that the meat was not yet ready to be served. And then the sage continued to talk.

By then, the sultan had lost all patience. His hunger pains were unbearable. He couldn't think or talk. So he got up to see what was taking so long. He was surprised to see the pots of meat on one side of the room. And the fires on the other side of the room.

The sultan asked, "How can the meat cook? The pots are not over the fire."

The sage told him not to worry. "There's no problem at all," he said.

The sultan became angry. "I don't understand!" he exclaimed. "How on earth can you cook the meat this way? I say you can't. It's impossible!"

The sage nodded. "You're right," he said at last. "It is impossible."

The frustrated sultan shook his fist. He demanded, "Then why are you doing this?"

The sage replied, "To teach you a lesson. You see, the meat and the pots are just like that young man and his wife. How could a fire on the shore of Shela protect someone on the shore of Manda?"

The sultan finally understood. He realized that the sage had taught him a valuable lesson. It had not been fair to take the rich merchant's side. Especially when the merchant was not being true to his word.

The sultan agreed that the young man had earned the 100 dollars. And he quickly ordered the merchant to pay him.

The young man was very grateful to the sage. He tried to give him one-third of the money. But the sage would not accept the fee.

This is the story of the lion of Manda.

A Tale from Angola

The Frog Takes a Bride

A YOUNG EARTHLY man had fallen in love. He loved the daughter of Lord Sun and Lady Moon. As was the custom, he wrote a letter to the girl's parents. In it, he asked for her hand in marriage.

But there was just one problem. You see, the girl lived in Heaven. There had been a ladder between Heaven and Earth. But it was no longer in place. Now there was no way for the man to send his letter.

The young man called upon all the animals and all the birds of Earth. He asked, "Can any of you deliver my letter?"

The lion said no. The elephant said no. And the eagle said no.

But Mainu the Frog gave a different answer. "I can do it," he said. "I can deliver your letter."

The young man found this hard to believe. How could Mainu the Frog get to Heaven? Even the eagle could not!

So the man dismissed the frog's offer. And he sadly walked away.

Mainu wanted to prove his cleverness. So he stole the letter. And he prepared it for delivery.

You see, Mainu knew that the People of the Sun often came down to Earth. They traveled on Spider's long cobweb. They visited to draw water at a very special well.

Mainu had seen the People of the Sun do this many times. So he knew where the well was. He went straight there. And he waited.

Sure enough, Spider's long cobweb came down from Heaven. And the People of the Sun came down to draw water. When the first water jar was lowered into the well, Mainu jumped in. And he was carried to Heaven.

Mainu quickly delivered the letter to Lord Sun. No one saw him do it.

Lord Sun read the letter. He was puzzled. He ordered his subjects to search for the suitor. But Mainu had already jumped into another water jar and gone back to Earth.

Mainu told the young man what he had done. He told him that he would return to Heaven the next day. And he would find out Lord Sun's response to the letter.

The next day, Mainu arrived in Heaven just in time. He heard Lord Sun say, "I will approve of this marriage between my daughter and her unknown suitor. But only if the young man shows himself to me. He must also bring forth a gift—a large sack of money."

Mainu quickly returned to Earth. He went to the young man. "You must show yourself to Lord Sun," he said. "Let's go!"

Now the young man could not fit inside a water jar. So he could not travel to Heaven.

"Lord Sun and Lady Moon will never approve of me," he fretted. "They won't want their daughter to marry an Earthly man."

Of course, Mainu had a plan. "Don't

worry, young man," he said. "Give me a sack of money. And I will present it to Lord Sun for you. And soon, you will have your bride."

The young man trusted Mainu. So Mainu took the gift and jumped into another water jar.

When Mainu reached Heaven, he placed the gift at the foot of Lord Sun's bed. He then hid himself in the girl's room. While she slept, he stole both her eyes!

And Mainu returned to Earth.

The next morning, Lord Sun and Lady Moon discovered the sack of money. Then they saw what had happened to their daughter.

Quickly, they consulted a sage. "What has happened to our daughter?" they wailed.

The sage explained. "Your daughter's suitor has cast a spell on her. If she is not taken to him soon, she will die."

Lord Sun and Lady Moon called Spider. "Weave us a thick cobweb," they ordered. And the girl traveled to Earth to meet her suitor.

Meanwhile, Mainu had given the girl's eyes to the young man. "She will join you," Mainu said.

When the girl arrived, her suitor

returned her eyes. And soon they were married.

After that, the girl never returned to her Heavenly home. But the frog had the power to go back and forth. And that is why it is said that frogs sometimes fall from the sky in rainstorms.

A BRAVE TORTOISE

THE RAINS WERE late. And the entire countryside was very, very dry. The animals could only get water by licking the mud in the nearby riverbed. The people were dying because there was no water.

The sun showed no pity. He seemed to enjoy burning up the land below.

The old men of the village gathered to discuss the problem.

"The spirit of the river must be angry with us," they said. They decided to give the river a gift. But what kind of gift do you give a river?

A little herd boy listened to the old men talk. He ran to the river. "I'll give it a gift," he said.

First, the boy offered his father's best black ox. It was the one that his father bragged about.

The river refused the gift by making no movement.

The little boy then offered his father's favorite cow. It was the one that had produced much milk and many calves.

Again, the spirit of the river stayed quiet. And it stirred up the dust in its riverbed.

The boy was sad. He was completely out of ideas. Then he thought of his sister. The little girl was filled with laughter and song.

The boy offered her as a gift. And the spirit of the river bubbled up with fresh water. There was enough in the pool for all to drink.

All the people drank to their hearts' content. Then the little boy headed home. He knew he had to fulfill his promise to the river.

"Hello, sister," he said when he found her.

"Hello, brother," she replied happily.

The boy asked, "How would you like to play with me by the river?"

"What fun!" she cried.

The two children skipped to the river. They played for the rest of the day. And the little girl laughed and sang the whole time.

At the end of the day, the little girl became

very tired. She fell asleep under a tree near the river's edge. Her brother quickly ran away.

When the girl awoke, the spirit of the river had risen up from the water. It was about to claim her!

The girl was frightened by the strange, watery sight. She screamed. And she ran away as fast as she could. She didn't even look back.

Well, the girl didn't pay attention to her path. Soon she was lost. And she was scared.

"How will I ever get home?" she cried.

Night was falling. The girl spotted a nice cornfield. She looked for a farmhouse. But there wasn't one.

The girl didn't know that she had wandered out of her own land. Now she was in the animal kingdom that belonged to King Elephant.

The little girl was very hungry. So she gathered some ripe corn for her meal.

Her legs were weary from running so fast and so far. She made a shelter from the thick bushes. She gathered twigs for a small fire. She covered herself with some leaves. And she fell fast asleep.

At sunrise, the little girl awoke to the sound of King Elephant's servants. They were collecting the ripe corn.

She was lying in the thick bushes. So she was not seen.

The little girl overheard the servants talking. One of them said, "We must alert King Elephant at once!"

"What is the matter?" asked another.

"A thief has stolen some of King Elephant's corn!"

With that, the servants ran to King Elephant's side. They reported the missing corn. And the king immediately called upon the jackal.

"Go kill the thief," ordered King Elephant.

The jackal went into the field. Nervously, he looked for the thief. He yelled out a warning. "Come out so I may kill you!"

The little girl was well hidden in the thick bushes. She heard the jackal's request. She disguised her voice. And she pretended to be much bigger than she really was.

"Go away!" she shouted. "I am a big creature—much bigger than you are! I have sharp horns as large as the trees. And I have large, pointy teeth. I could easily crush you and eat you!"

The jackal heard this. In fear, he stopped searching. Instead, he ran back to King Elephant without delay.

The jackal warned all the animals about the creature in the bush. He said, "The creature is even bigger than King Elephant!"

There was a great silence among the animals. King Elephant did not know what to say or do. He believed the jackal. He flapped his huge ears while he thought.

"We can't let that creature eat all of our food," he sighed.

Suddenly, a voice was heard from the crowd of animals. It was a strong voice. "I can rid the land of the thief," he boomed.

The animals looked around. "Who's there?" someone asked.

The voice got louder. And the animals realized that the tortoise was the one who was speaking so bravely.

The tortoise continued speaking. Then he strutted down the path toward the field. The other animals cheered him on. It seemed that the tortoise was the only animal brave enough to defend the land.

Soon, the little girl heard the tortoise coming near. She became afraid. She could hear the loud rattling of his shell. And she could hear his booming voice.

The little girl was so afraid that she could no longer hide in the bushes. She dashed out and ran away as fast as she could.

The tortoise saw the girl running away. He felt proud. He also laughed at how cowardly the jackal had been. "The jackal was frightened by a little girl!" he chuckled.

The tortoise did not tell the other animals the whole truth.

"I have rid the field of the nasty creature that was stealing our corn," he boasted. "It was very large. And very ugly. But I chased it away for good!"

King Elephant was grateful to the tortoise. He announced, "You have been very brave. So I will make you my chief counselor."

The jackal, however, was banished from the land. King Elephant declared, "You are nothing but a coward!"

And ever since that time, the jackal has not had the courage to hunt for himself. Instead, he just follows the lion and eats his scraps.

The Singing Barrel

ONE DAY, A young girl was with her friends on the seashore. She found a beautiful shell.

"I'm going to search for more shells," said the girl. And she placed the first shell on a rock.

When it was time to go home, the girl forgot all about the beautiful shell. She was halfway home when she remembered. She asked her friends to walk back with her. But they all refused. So she went back alone.

The girl was a little scared to walk alone so close to nightfall. So she began to sing loudly. This took her mind off her fears.

Once the girl reached the rock, she discovered a fairy. It was sitting next to the beautiful shell.

The fairy had heard the girl's beautiful voice. And he asked, "Could you sing one more song for me?"

"Sure," said the girl. But as soon as she began to sing, the fairy grabbed her. He stuffed her inside a barrel. Then he nailed the barrel shut!

The fairy traveled from village to village. He entertained people in exchange for a good meal. Whenever the fairy beat the barrel like a drum, the girl sang. And the fairy would receive plenty of food. Of course, he never shared any of it with the girl.

The fairy traveled far and wide. Finally, he reached the girl's own village. The villagers were excited about the fairy's arrival. By this time, he was known throughout the land. Everyone had heard about the beautiful music that came from inside his barrel.

The fairy banged upon the barrel. When the girl sang, her parents recognized her voice.

"That is our daughter," said the mother.

"Yes, it is," agreed the father. "We will rescue her tonight."

The girl's parents offered to feed the fairy. He gladly accepted. He also accepted the wine they poured for him. He drank many glasses of it. After a while, the fairy fell asleep. Right during dessert!

The girl's parents acted quickly. They opened the barrel and freed their daughter. Then they filled the barrel with soldier ants and bees.

The next time the fairy beat the barrel, he did not hear beautiful music. He was badly stung instead!

Ananse Goes to Work

IT WAS PLANTING season again. Ananse the Spider told his wife, "Go and measure out some nuts. I'd like to plant them in our fields."

Ananse's wife did just that. Soon they were ready. And Ananse took his hoe and walked out to the fields. He searched a long time for a shady place to rest. He found a nice spot by a cool stream.

Now Ananse was a lazy spider. He preferred to have someone else do his work. So he just relaxed by the stream. He drank the cool water. And he ate the nuts. When all the nuts were gone, Ananse fell asleep.

In the evening, Ananse woke up. He took some mud from the stream. And he rubbed it all over his body.

Ananse returned home. "I worked so hard today," he lied. "Look how dirty I got."

"Good for you, dear," said Ananse's wife. "Why don't you go take a bath. I'll fix a nice dinner for you. You deserve a reward for all of your hard work."

Each day after that, Ananse went out to the fields. And each day, he found another shady spot. At every sunset, he covered himself with mud and went home. His wife was very proud of him.

One day, Ananse's wife said, "It is gathering time, Ananse. It is time to dig up our nuts. Since you have worked so hard this season, I will do it. You just stay home and rest today."

Ananse quickly answered, "No, my wife. I enjoy working in the fields. And I would not want to sit still while you dig up the nuts I planted. I will go and dig them up myself. It is the only right thing to do."

Ananse's wife did not argue.

"What can I do?" Ananse wondered. He decided to steal nuts from his neighbor's field.

So very early the next morning, Ananse crept to his neighbor's field. And he stole some nuts. Later in the day, he proudly took the nuts home. He bragged to his wife about his hard work.

Ananse's wife was very impressed with the large crop of nuts. And she was pleased with Ananse's attitude.

Ananse stole from his neighbor every day for a week.

The neighbor vowed he would catch the thief. So he got up early one morning. And he hid near his field.

Shortly, the neighbor spotted Ananse. "I should have known it was that lazy Ananse," he muttered. "I'll trap him!" he declared.

The neighbor got to work. He made a figure out of sticks. Then he covered the sticks with the sticky gum of the rubber tree. In the dark, the figure looked just like a man.

The next day, Ananse got up early as usual. The sun had not yet come up. As Ananse arrived at the neighbor's field, he saw the shadowy figure. It looked like a man to Ananse.

Someone else must be stealing from my neighbor's field! thought Ananse. Ananse bravely approached the man.

"Why are you standing in my way?" demanded Ananse.

The gummy man did not answer.

"I said, why are you standing in my way?"

Again, the gummy man did not answer.

Ananse was becoming angry at the gummy man's silence. He said, "If you do not answer me, I will have to use force! If I were you, I'd run away!"

Well, the gummy man did not answer. And he did not run away. So Ananse gave him a push with his right hand. His hand stuck! But Ananse didn't realize it right away.

"Oh, so you are being stubborn!" Ananse shouted. He tried to push the gummy man with his left hand. That hand stuck too.

In his fury, Ananse kicked the gummy man. First with his right foot. And then his left. Both feet became stuck.

Finally, Ananse hit the gummy man with

his head. You guessed it. Ananse's head stuck to the figure! And the harder Ananse wiggled, the more stuck he became.

The neighbor had been watching the whole thing. Once Ananse was completely stuck, the neighbor came out of hiding.

The neighbor pulled Ananse off the gummy figure. He dragged him toward the village.

"The chief will judge you," he said.

As Ananse was dragged through town, the villagers laughed and jeered. Ananse was so ashamed of being caught. And he tried to wiggle free several times.

But it was no use. Ananse couldn't get away.

A judgment was quickly passed on Ananse's crime. The chief said, "You will pay your neighbor for the crops you've stolen."

Ananse pleaded with the chief. "Please let me go home," he said. "I can return with the money today."

The chief knew how tricky Ananse the Spider could be. The chief agreed to let Ananse go home on one condition. "Only if your neighbor and I go with you," he said.

So Ananse, the neighbor, and the chief began to walk to Ananse's house. Halfway there, Ananse broke free from the chief's grasp. And he fled down the road.

Ananse ran into the first house he came to. He crawled into the rafters. And he hid in the darkest corner he could find. Ananse the Spider was never heard from again!

Next time you see a spider hiding in a corner, say hello. It just might be Ananse!

A Yoruba Tale from Nigeria

How the Goat Came to the Village

IN THE BEGINNING, all the animals drank from the same pool of water. The pool was very large. And the water was always cool and plentiful.

Once a year, the animals liked to thank the pool of water for being so generous. The animals would all gather at the pool. And they would give it a good cleaning.

The water served all the animals. So the council of animals set a very strict rule. If any animal did not help clean the pool, that animal would be killed.

Well, Goat did not show up to clean the pool one year. It was said that Goat had a new baby kid. And she did not want to leave the kid by himself.

The other animals were angry. Many of them had brought their babies to pool-cleaning day. They didn't believe that Goat should miss it just because she had a new kid. So they sent messengers to question her.

Goat had overheard the meeting of the animals. She knew about the messengers. She also knew about the awful rule. So she prepared herself.

Stag was the first messenger. He demanded a reason for Goat's absence.

"I have a new kid," Goat answered politely.

"Is the kid male or female?" asked Stag.

Goat knew that Stag's mother had died recently. So she said her kid was female.

Stag then asked whose mother had been born again in the kid.

"It is your mother," Goat replied.

Now Stag could not harm Goat. Not if his own mother had been reborn as Goat's kid. So he let Goat live.

Next, the animals sent Antelope.

"I have a new kid," Goat politely told Antelope.

Antelope demanded to know whether Goat's kid was male or female.

Goat remembered that Antelope's father had recently died. So Goat told Antelope that the kid was male.

Antelope then asked Goat whose father had been reborn in her kid.

"It's your father," Goat replied.

Antelope knew that he could not harm Goat now. So he let Goat live.

Many of the other animals went one by one to ask Goat the same questions. Each animal just happened to have a parent who had died recently. Goat knew about each of the deaths. And she told the animals that her kid was their parent reborn. Each animal let Goat live.

Leopard had become very suspicious of Goat. He thought that perhaps Goat was playing a trick on all the animals. So Leopard hid behind the bushes and listened as the animals visited her.

Leopard figured out what Goat was doing. And he decided to visit her himself.

Leopard walked up to Goat. He demanded to know why she had not shown up for the cleaning of the pool.

"I have a new kid," Goat answered politely.

"Is the kid male or female?" Leopard demanded.

Goat knew that Leopard's mother had died. So she said that the kid was female.

Leopard then asked whose mother had been born again in her kid.

"It is your mother," Goat told Leopard.

Leopard said, "You know, it could have been my father. He died at the same time my mother did. You know, I loved my father far more than I loved my mother."

When Goat tried to change her story, Leopard jumped at her. And he let out a very loud roar.

Goat jumped sideways out of her house. She ran as fast as she could. Leopard followed right behind her.

When Leopard had chased Goat into the Village of Men, he stopped. Then he turned around and went back home.

Goat has lived there ever since. She knows that all leopards eat goats who stray from their village.

A Tale from West Africa

The Snake and the Flea

THERE WAS ONCE a girl named Sirabela. She was very beautiful. And she knew it.

When she was old enough, Sirabela tried to pick a husband. But it was very hard.

Many men proposed to Sirabela. Each one of them was turned down. Why? Because Sirabela was waiting for a better man.

There was one young man named Tokko. He loved Sirabela very much. But because he was poor, Sirabela would not even consider marrying him.

Meanwhile, Minia had heard about the

beautiful Sirabela. So he came to the village to marry her.

Neither Sirabela nor the villagers knew that Minia was really a snake. He had magically changed himself into a young prince.

Sirabela was so taken with Minia's riches that she eagerly agreed to marry him.

The young couple traveled with the wedding party to Minia's village. This is where the wedding was to take place. The journey took several days. The wedding party came to a river. And they got into a boat and rowed across.

On the other side, the land looked different. It was no longer green and bright. It was dark and dreary. But the wedding party was busy having a good time. So no one noticed the changes.

The party followed Minia into a huge forest. It was filled with thousands of tall, dark trees. The forest was so thick that there was just one small entrance to it. That entrance led to Minia's kingdom.

The wedding party was still having a good time. They did not notice that the forest was thick. Or that the entrance was small. The party trusted the rich young prince. And they followed him right into his kingdom.

Once inside, Minia changed back into a snake. He then wrapped himself around a large tree and blocked the entrance.

Sirabela was shocked. And frightened. She did not know what to do.

Everyone tried to calm her by singing songs and telling tales. But Sirabela could not stop thinking about her future husband—the snake.

"Why won't you let us go?" she cried at length.

"Never! You're mine now," answered Minia.

"But what about my friends and my family? You don't need them."

Minia thought about it for a moment. Then he agreed. One by one, he began to release the storytellers, the singers, and all the rest.

Now, Sirabela had a plan. She could also change into other things. So she changed herself into a flower.

Sirabela's sister waited in line to be released. Minia told her that she could go. "But only if you give me the flower in your hair," he said.

Sirabela burst into tears as she changed from the flower back into a girl.

Later, Sirabela's sister stood in line again.

When it was her turn, Minia told her that she could go. "But only if you leave behind the ring that's on your finger," he said.

And Sirabela burst into tears as she changed from the ring back into a girl.

Later still, Sirabela's sister stood in line. This time Minia studied her from head to toe. He could find nothing different about the girl. So he had no choice but to release her.

Outside the kingdom, Sirabela changed back into a girl. She was free! She and her sister jumped for joy.

You see, Sirabela had changed into a flea. She had hidden in her sister's hair with the other fleas. Minia had no idea which flea might be her. So Sirabela was saved.

When Sirabela got home, she realized how foolish she had been.

"I think I will marry a man for his goodness and not for his riches," she decided.

Sirabela wed Tokko the very next day. The village rejoiced. They had a great feast for the young couple.

And Sirabela was happy. Because she knew that her husband was a real prince among men.

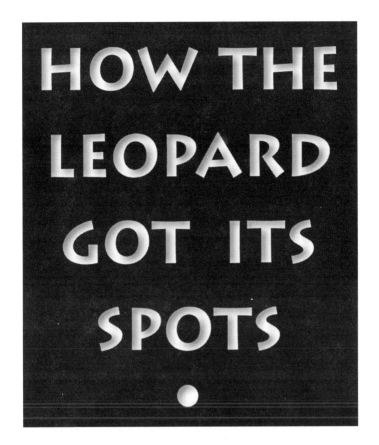

HOW THE LEOPARD GOT ITS SPOTS

IN THE BEGINNING, Leopard and Fire were the very best of friends. Every day, Leopard visited Fire at his home. But Fire never went to Leopard's house to visit.

Leopard's wife questioned her husband's friendship with Fire. Each evening she asked, "When is Fire coming over to visit? It is customary to return a visit from a friend."

Leopard grew tired of hearing his wife complain about this. He didn't really mind visiting Fire's home. In fact, he liked it. It was quite pleasant and warm. But because of his wife's questions, Leopard started to notice something.

"Hmmmm," he said one day. "It is strange. Fire never even mentions leaving his own home. And he certainly never suggests visiting my home."

Leopard decided to extend a formal invitation to Fire. "Come visit me at my house," he said.

Fire answered with many excuses. But Leopard had an answer for every excuse. This left Fire with no choice. He had to accept the invitation.

Fire told Leopard that he had never walked before. But he could visit if there was a path of dry leaves from his house to Leopard's.

Leopard agreed to make the path. And he asked Fire to visit the next day.

Leopard's wife was so excited. She helped make the path. Then she and Leopard cleaned the house and prepared a large meal for their friend. They wanted to make sure that Fire's first visit was pleasant.

"We want him to feel welcome," said Leopard's wife. "That way, maybe he'll visit again."

The next day, Leopard and his wife waited for Fire to arrive. They heard the wind stirring strongly. And they heard loud crackling sounds. It all sounded like it was right outside their door.

Leopard got up to see what was the matter. When he opened the door, there stood Fire. He was extending his hand.

"Thank you for the invitation," he said sincerely.

Leopard reached out to grasp Fire's hand. When Fire's fingers of flame touched Leopard, he screamed in pain. And Leopard and his wife jumped out the window.

Their house was totally destroyed. And ever since that time, Leopard and his wife have had black spots all over their bodies. For that is where Fire touched them.

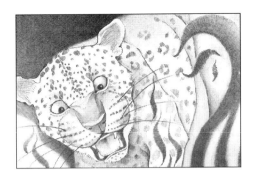

The Play

HOW THE LEOPARD GOT ITS SPOTS

Cast of Characters

Narrator

Leopard's Wife

Leopard

Fire

Setting: An African village where animals live

Act I

Narrator: This is the tale of how Leopard got his spots. In the beginning, Leopard and Fire were very good friends. One day, Leopard prepared to go visit his friend Fire.

Leopard's Wife: Where are you going, Leopard?

Leopard: I am on my way to visit my good friend Fire.

Leopard's Wife: Again?! You are going to visit Fire. And yet he has never paid you a visit. This is not proper, my husband. Why do you go there?

Leopard: I like Fire. He is my friend. I enjoy talking with him. I really don't see the problem, my wife.

Leopard's Wife: A true friend repays the visit of another friend. That is our custom. Why can't Fire visit you here? Is our home so untidy? Is Fire too good to come here?

Leopard: No, that is not it. I have never even invited him.

Leopard's Wife: Never invited him? Why not?! Are you ashamed of our home? Do you think that Fire is too good to come here? Are you ashamed of me?!

Leopard: No, no, that is not it. I did not know how important this was for you. I tell you what. When I visit Fire today, I will invite him to our home. You will see. Then you can stop your fussing.

Narrator: Leopard walked outside. He wondered how he would approach Fire with the invitation.

Act II

Narrator: Leopard and Fire were talking in Fire's cozy home. Leopard finally got up enough courage to invite Fire over.

Leopard: Fire, my wife has a silly idea. She thinks that you don't think our home is worthy enough to visit. I told her that she was wrong. And that I would invite you to our home. Will you come to dinner? That way, she will no longer think that you are impolite.

Fire: My good friend! Please tell your wife that I am sure your home is a very nice place. But I don't visit many places. I try to stay home most of the time.

Leopard: But Fire, this is very important to me. My wife will not stop talking about it. Worse than that, she may stop me from coming to visit you. Is it at all possible for you to come? Just once—to quiet her down?

Fire: You do not understand, Leopard. I don't visit well. I am afraid that your wife will not like me. If it would make her feel better, invite her to come here. And I will prepare a wonderful warm meal for her. I'll show her my hospitality.

Leopard: No thanks, Fire. That is very nice of you. But it will not satisfy her. She says that it is against our custom not to repay a visit from a friend. She wants you to cross our threshold. Please. Visit our home just once. I will never ask you to do it again.

Fire: It is not that easy for me to get around.

Leopard: What do you mean?

Fire: I do not walk. In order for me to travel, a path has to be made.

Leopard: Well, just tell me what to do. And I will help make your journey to my house easier.

Fire: I will need a path of dry leaves—from my house to your house. That is the only way I will be able to visit. If it is too much trouble, I will gladly stay home.

Leopard: That is no trouble at all. I will be happy to make the path for you. I will have it ready by tomorrow. You can come then.

Fire: All right, my friend. I will see you tomorrow.

Narrator: Leopard was very happy. He ran home to tell his wife the good news.

Act III

Narrator: Leopard and his wife busily cleaned their home. They were nervous about Fire's first visit. Leopard's wife wanted to make a good impression. So she cooked a big meal.

Leopard's Wife: I gathered as many dry leaves as I could find.

Leopard: Thank you, my wife. It was quite enough. I was able to make a very thick path for Fire to follow.

Leopard's Wife: I wonder why Fire needs a path to get here. Didn't you give him directions? Did he explain to you why he needs the leaves?

Leopard: I gave him very clear directions. He did say, though, that he doesn't walk. Maybe he thought the leaves would help him stay on the right path.

Leopard's Wife: Maybe. It must be getting close to the time for his visit.

Leopard: Yes, he must be on his way. I am looking forward to this. He is such a warm friend.

Narrator: Leopard and his wife finished their preparations. Then they sat at the window and waited for a knock at the door.

Suddenly, Leopard and his wife were frightened. They heard awful noises coming from outside. The wind was blowing so hard. Their house was shaking. And there were loud crackling noises that sounded like thunder.

Leopard's Wife: What is that noise outside?

Leopard: I don't know. I hope it will not stop Fire from making his visit today.

Leopard's Wife: Go look outside. See what is going on.

Narrator: Leopard walked to the door. When he opened it, there stood his friend. Fire was blazing brightly in front of him.

Fire: Hello, my friend. It was a lovely stroll over here. Quick too. I am so happy that you invited me for a visit. Is this your lovely wife?

Narrator: Fire extended both of his hands to his hosts. Leopard and his wife reached out to him in kind. But as soon as they touched him, they jumped back quickly. His grip was hot!

Leopard's home went up in flames. Luckily, Leopard and his wife were able to jump out the window. And they ran far, far away.

But Leopard and his wife were forever marked on the places that Fire touched them. And that is how the leopard got its spots.